CONTENTS

the ultimate

DreamWorks

Shrek ®

Annual
2006

DreamWorks
ANIMATION SKG

Pedigree ®

Published by Pedigree Books Limited
Beech Hill House, Walnut Gardens, Exeter EX4 4DH
Email books@pedigreegroup.co.uk
Published in 2005

£6.99

Shrek

Shrek is a big, green, smelly ogre who enjoys taking mud showers and eating forest critters. Perfectly content living alone in his swamp, he scares the spit out of anyone who crosses his path. It takes a princess that packs a punch to soften his heart and change him in ways no one thought ogrely possible.

Donkey

Donkey's got a mouth that just won't quit, but he's no jackass – inside he has the heart of a noble steed. As Shrek's unlikely sidekick, he's always up for a royal quest and along the way he finds true friendship, as well as a hot romance. But eventually Donkey faces a quest of his own – in order to remain Shrek's best friend, he has to deal with some unexpected competition.

Princess Fiona

Princess Fiona is smart, tough and spirited and can drop-kick a band of outlaws with the best of them. While she tries to stick with the fairytale conventions, she is not your typical damsel in distress. She harbours a deep, dark secret, as she waits patiently for her one true love to sweep her off her feet.

Puss In Boots

He has the steely eyes of a killer, swashbuckling finesse and really expensive Corinthian footwear. He's Puss In Boots, the famed ogre killer of myth and song. He's been hired to do a hit on Shrek, only to discover his victim to be a great adversary and – ultimately – an even greater friend.

Dragon

She may breathe fire but this is no ordinary fairytale dragon. Hanging out at the fiery keep, surrounded by boiling lava all day long can make any dragon hungry for a little action. Look out for dragon and donkey's new offspring Dronkeys!

Lord Farquaad

Lord Farquaad, the four-foot-tall ruler of Duloc was a power-hungry control freak, who wanted to rid his land of all the undesirable fairytale creatures. To become a king he needed to marry a princess and he decided that Fiona would make the perfect bride. But first he needed to rescue her from the Dragon's Keep - although he was not prepared to undertake such a dangerous quest himself.

Queen Lillian

Queen Lillian, Fiona's mother, was shocked to find her daughter is now a full-time ogress with an ogre for a husband. But the queen is willing to see beyond appearances as all she wants is a little family harmony.

King Harold

King Harold thought he was doing his best for Fiona by making a deal with the Fairy Godmother – she told him to lock the Princess in a tower to await the kiss of Prince Charming. The King was unhappy to find that Fiona's husband is an ogre, instead of the handsome prince he was expecting. But the King, too, is not quite what one might expect.

The Fairy Godmother

As the mother of Prince Charming, Fiona's intended husband, the Fairy Godmother is furious when she finds out that the Princess is already married. She blames the King for the fact that their plan did not work out as she had hoped, and is determined to get rid of Shrek so her son can claim his bride.

Prince Charming

Prince Charming looks like every girl's dream date, but appearances can be deceptive. He had planned to marry Princess Fiona, but when he arrived at the Dragon's Keep to rescue her, he found he was too late and a wolf had taken her place in the tower. Nevertheless, with his mother's help.

The Quest

Once upon a time there was a lovely princess, but she had an enchantment upon her of a fearful sort which could only be broken by love's first kiss. She was locked away in a castle, guarded by a terrible fire-breathing dragon. Many brave knights had attempted to free her from this dreadful prison, but none prevailed. She waited in the Dragon's Keep in the highest room of the tallest tower for her true love and true love's first kiss.

"Like that's ever going to happen," said Shrek, tearing a page from the book to use as toilet paper, "What a load of..."

He took a mud shower and squeezed a bug onto his toothbrush, before enjoying another quiet day at his shack in the swamp. His evening meal of eyeballs was interrupted by a group of townspeople, armed with pitchforks, who had come to hunt the ogre. Shrek crept up behind them as they approached his shack. "Arrrhhh!" he roared. "This is the part where you run away," he added in a whisper, as they cowered, petrified.

As the men fled, they dropped a poster. Shrek picked it up. "Wanted. Fairytale Creatures. Reward," he read.

The following day, there was a long queue of people waiting to hand over all manner of fairytale creatures and claim their rewards. As knights loaded the creatures into crates for relocation, an old lady joined the queue with a talking donkey.

"Please don't turn me in. I'll never be stubborn again," pleaded Donkey. "I can change, give me another chance."

"Ten shillings for the talking donkey, if you can prove it talks," said a knight. For once in his life, Donkey managed to keep silent.

"Get out of my sight," the knight told the old lady.

Suddenly some magic fairy dust hit Donkey on the head and he started to fly through the air. "Hey, I can fly!" he exclaimed. As the magic wore off, he fell to the ground.

"Seize him!" shouted the knight. Donkey ran into the forest, pursued by a group of knights, and found himself face to butt with Shrek.

"I am authorised, by the order of Lord Farquaad, to place you both under arrest and transport you to a designated resettlement facility," declared one of the knights.

"Oh really," said Shrek, sarcastically. "You and what army?"

The knight glanced behind him to find the others had fled. He turned and ran.

"Man it's good to be free," said Donkey.

"Why don't you go and celebrate your freedom with your own friends," Shrek suggested, walking away.

"I don't have any friends," Donkey told him, "and I'm not going out there by myself! I've got a great idea. I'll stick with you! I like you! You gotta let me stay!"

"One night only," Shrek finally agreed reluctantly. "Outside!"

As Shrek was eating his supper, he heard a noise. "I thought I told you to stay outside," he shouted to Donkey.

"I am outside," Donkey replied.

To his horror, Shrek found that his shack had been invaded by the fairytale creatures evicted by Lord Farquaad.

"I'm a terrifying ogre," he yelled, "what do I have to do to get a little privacy?" As he opened the door to throw the creatures out, he saw that his swamp was overrun by refugees.

"Who knows where this Farquaad guy is?" Shrek demanded.

"I do! Me! Me! Pick me!" Donkey shouted, jumping up and down.

"Okay," said Shrek, "You're coming with me."

Meanwhile in Duloc, Thelonius was torturing a gingerbread man by dipping him in a glass of milk.

"That's enough," said Farquaad, "he's ready to talk."

"You're a monster," the gingerbread man spluttered.

"You're the monster," Farquaad replied. "You and the rest of that fairytale trash, poisoning my perfect world.

"Now tell me, where are the others?" he demanded, reaching for one of the gingerbread man's gumdrop buttons.

The gingerbread man was spared by the arrival of a knight, who unveiled a mirror.

Lord Farquaad addressed the magic mirror, "Mirror, mirror, on the wall, is this not the most perfect kingdom of them all?" he asked. "Well," the mirror replied tentatively, "technically you're not a king... but you can become one.

All you have to do is marry a princess. So just sit back and relax my lord. It's time for you to meet today's eligible bachelorettes.

"Bachelorette number one is a

shut-in from a kingdom far, far away. She likes sushi, and hot-tubbing anytime! Her hobbies include cooking and cleaning for her two evil sisters! Please welcome Cinderella

"Bachelorette number two is a cape-wearing girl from the land of fancy. Just kiss her dead, frozen lips and find out what a live wire she is! Give it up for Snow White.

"Bachelorette number three is a fiery redhead from a dragon-guarded castle surrounded by boiling lava, but don't let that cool you off! She's a loaded pistol who likes Piña Coladas and getting caught in the rain. Yours for the rescuing... Princess Fiona!"

"Um, well, OK, uuuhhh... number three!" said Farquaad. "Princess Fiona. She's perfect! All I have to do is find someone to rescue her. I know, we'll hold a tournament!"

Shrek and Donkey arrived in Duloc on Tournament Day to find the place deserted. Then they heard Farquaad's voice, coming from the stadium.

"Brave knights! You are the best and brightest in the land – and today one of you will prove himself better and brighter than the rest! That champion shall have the honour to rescue the lovely Princess Fiona from the fiery keep of the dragon! Some of you may die, but it's a sacrifice I am willing to make!"

Shrek marched straight through the row of knights, and stood defiantly in front of the podium.

"What is that?" shrieked Farquaad, looking at Shrek in horror, "It's hideous!"

"It's just a donkey!" retorted Shrek.

Farquaad considered for a second. "Knights, new plan! The one who kills the ogre will be champion!"

"Alright then. Come on!" Shrek challenged the knights. He started to work his way through them until he had floored them all. The crowd went wild. "Thank you very much," Shrek acknowledged their cheers.

"Congratulations, ogre, you've won the honour of embarking on a great and noble quest," Farquaad announced.

"Quest? I'm already on a quest," Shrek replied. "A quest to get my swamp back! My swamp where you dumped all those fairytale creatures."

"Alright ogre – I'll make you a deal. Go on a quest for me and I'll give you your swamp back!" Farquaad said.

Shrek and Donkey set out immediately on their quest to rescue Princess Fiona. As they headed for the dilapidated castle, the landscape was transformed into a bleak burnt-out wasteland.

Donkey sniffed the air in disgust, "Whew! Shrek! Did you do that?" Man! You gotta warn somebody before you just crack one off like that!

"Believe me, Donkey, if that was me you'd be dead," Shrek replied. "It's brimstone. We must be getting close."

They spotted the castle, set on a rock pinnacle amid a lake of molten lava. Shrek made for the rickety bridge, while Donkey peered reluctantly at the boiling lava below.

"You can't tell me you're afraid of heights," Shrek teased him. "Come on, we'll just tackle this thing together, one little baby step at a time. Just don't look down."

Donkey picked his way gingerly across the bridge, "Shrek, I'm looking down! You gotta let me go back," he cried, as a slat fell into the lava below.

"But you're already halfway," Shrek reassured him.

"Yeah, but I know that half is safe," Donkey replied.

Suddenly Donkey realised he'd reached the other side. "Cool!" he said with new-found confidence. Then he whispered "You afraid?"

"No," Shrek replied, putting on some armour left behind by an unfortunate knight. "Now see if you can find any stairs. The Princess will be in the tallest tower. I read it in a book once."

Donkey headed off in search of a staircase, "Cool!" he said, "You handle the dragon, I'll handle the stairs!"

Suddenly Donkey found himself eyeball to eyeball with Dragon. He ran in the opposite direction, a fireball close behind him. As Dragon closed in on Donkey, Shrek grabbed her tail. She whipped her tail around, sending him hurtling into the air and clean through the window of the princess's bed chamber.

Now Donkey was trapped by Dragon.

"Why what large teeth you have...," he stuttered, "I mean white, sparkling teeth. I know you probably hear this all the time... from your food... that is one dazzling smile you've got there."

Donkey stumbled on as Dragon leered seductively, "You know what else? You're, you're a girl dragon. I mean, you're just reeking of feminine beauty! Hey, I'd just love to stick around, but I'm an asthmatic and I don't know if it'll work out, what with you blowing those smoke rings and stuff," Donkey coughed. "Shrek! Help! Shreeeekkk!"

Meanwhile, Princess Fiona took a quick peek at the intruder, before grabbing a bouquet and resuming her Sleeping Beauty pose. Suddenly, she found herself being shaken violently by the shoulders.

"Wake up!" yelled Shrek, "Are you Princess Fiona?"

Fiona composed herself before replying. "I am, awaiting a knight so bold as to rescue me."

"That's nice. Let's go." said Shrek, grabbing Fiona by the hand. As he dragged her through the castle, they heard a roar.

"You didn't slay the dragon?" shrieked Fiona. "It's on my to-do list," Shrek replied, hauling her down the stairs.

"Call me old-fashioned, but I don't want to rush into a physical relationship," jabbered Donkey, "uh, I'm not, ah, emotionally ready for a commitment of this magnitude!"

Shrek peered down at Donkey and Dragon and, seizing his opportunity, grabbed a chain holding a candelabra above Dragon's head.

"Hey, hey, what are you doing?" asked Donkey. "Okay, okay, look let's just back up a little and take things one step at a time. I mean, we really should get to know each other first... as friends,

or maybe even as pen pals... 'cause I'm on the road a lot, but I just love receiving cards..."

Dragon moved in to kiss Donkey as he continued to splutter his excuses, "Hey, you know, I'd really like to stay but..."

Suddenly Shrek fell, landing on top of Donkey and taking Dragon's kiss right on his butt. The dragon was even more shocked than Shrek. She reared up and blasted fireballs as the candelabra fell down around her neck. Shrek raced through the hall with Donkey and Fiona under his arms and the dragon in hot pursuit, trailing the chain of the candelabra behind her.

Shrek grabbed a sword from a dead knight. "Okay you two, head for the exit, I'll take care of the dragon." As Dragon chased after them, he jammed the sword through one of the links in the chain and made a run for it. Shrek caught up with Donkey and Fiona and they just made it to the bridge as a fireball swept after them. As they crossed, the fireball set fire to the bridge behind them. The lovesick dragon burst through the flames, but suddenly the chain tightened, stopping her in mid-flight. The bridge broke, but Shrek, Donkey and Fiona managed to climb up the slats to safety.

Shrek's Guide to Elegant Entertaining swamp Style

First Impressions

Make your guests feel welcome from the moment they arrive.

Ambiance

Use candles to create a warm cozy atmosphere.

Table settings

Lay the cutlery on the table in order of use, starting from the outside. A set of matching placemats (see opposite) will enhance your dining experience.

Pets

Lock pets away so they don't disturb your guests while they are eating.

How to make a Shrek place mat

Trace or copy the design opposite onto a sheet of A4 paper and colour it in. Cover it with a sheet of sticky-backed plastic, or slide it into a transparent plastic folder for a wipe-clean finish. Why not make a set of monster mats for the whole family.

See page 49 for some delicious swamp side recipe ideas

Swamp Buddies Hide and Seek

Can you find the fairytale characters hiding in Shrek's swamp?

For Better or Worse

"You did it! You rescued me! You're amazing, you're wonderful, you're... a little unorthodox, I'll admit, but... thy deed is great and thine heart is pure. I am eternally in your debt!" gushed Fiona. "The battle is won," she continued. "You may remove your helmet, good sir knight."

Shrek stalled for a minute, "Ahhh... no. I... I have helmet hair."

"Now remove your helmet!" Fiona ordered.

"Okay! Easy. As you command, Your Highness..." he added, removing the helmet.

"You're... an ogre?!" Fiona stuttered, staring at him blankly.

"Oh, you were expecting Prince Charming?" asked Shrek, giving her a long-suffering look. "Princess, I was sent to rescue you by Lord Farquaad, okay? He's the one who wants to marry you."

"Well, I'm sorry. You can tell Lord Farquaad that if he wants to rescue me properly I'll be waiting for him right here!" Fiona told him, determined not to move.

Throwing Fiona over his shoulder, Shrek set off. "You coming, Donkey?" he called.

Suddenly Fiona found herself dumped unceremoniously on the ground. "Shouldn't we stop to make camp?" she said nervously, looking at the setting sun, "There are robbers in the woods."

"Hey, come on, I'm scarier than anything we're gonna see in this forest," Shrek interrupted sarcastically.

"I NEED SOMEWHERE TO CAMP NOW!" Fiona yelled at him.

"Okay, over here!" Shrek called, rolling a boulder from the mouth of a cave.

"It's perfect!" said Fiona, ripping some bark off a nearby tree to make a door. "Well, Gentlemen, I bid thee goodnight."

"Hey Shrek... What we gonna do when we get our swamp back?" asked Donkey, as they gazed at the stars.

"There's no we," Shrek replied. "There's just me and my swamp. And the first thing I'm gonna do is build a ten-foot wall around my land."

"You cut me deep, Shrek, you cut me real deep..." said Donkey. "You know, I think this whole 'wall' thing is just a way to keep somebody out. What's your problem? What you got against the whole world?"

"Look, I'm not the one with the problem, okay? It's the world that seems to have a problem with me." Shrek sighed. "People take one look at me and go, 'Aaagh! Help! Run! A big, stupid, ugly ogre!' That's why I'm better off alone."

As they walked through the forest the next day Robin Hood suddenly swung down from a vine and grabbed Princess Fiona. "I am your saviour and I am rescuing you from this green beast," he said, kissing her hand. Fiona kicked Robin into the air and he landed against a rock, knocked out cold. Then, while arrows flew around her, Fiona did a back flip and took out the Merry Men, one by one, with a series of martial arts moves.

"Whoa, where did that come from?" asked Shrek, impressed.

"When one lives alone one has to learn these things," Fiona laughed nervously. "Hey, there's an arrow in your butt!"

Donkey started to panic, "Shrek's gonna die. You can't do this to me Shrek! Keep your legs elevated. Turn yer head and cough. Does anyone know the Heimlich?" Fiona decided to get rid of Donkey, and told him to go and look for a blue flower with red thorns.

"Blue flower, red thorns." Donkey repeated to himself as he searched in the forest. "OK I'm on it! Don't die Shrek. And if you see a long tunnel, STAY AWAY FROM THE LIGHT!"

Meanwhile, Fiona tried to remove the arrow. Just as Donkey raced round the corner, Fiona ripped the arrow from Shrek's butt. "Ooww!" he roared.

"Is that blood?" asked Donkey, passing out. Shrek picked him up and they continued on their way.

By late afternoon they had left the woods and Duloc stretched out before them. "There it is," said Shrek "I guess we better move on."

Fiona gave Shrek a meaningful glance, "But Shrek, I'm worried about Donkey. He doesn't

look so good."

Shrek suddenly caught on, "She's right. You look awful," he told Donkey. "Who's hungry? I'll find us some dinner."

"Mmm. Mmm. This is really good! What is this?" asked Fiona, when she tasted the food that Shrek had cooked.

"Weedrat. Rôtisserie-style," Shrek informed her proudly.

"They're also great in stews – I make a mean weedrat stew. Maybe you can come and visit me in the swamp sometime."

"Man," Donkey piped up, "isn't this romantic, just look at that sunset."

Fiona leapt to her feet, a desperate look on her face. "Sunset!! Oh no! I mean... it's late. I'd better go inside," she cried, heading for an old mill.

Donkey decided to follow Fiona into the mill. "Princess, where are you? It's very spooky in here..." he called out. Suddenly a huge ogress fell from above.

"Ahhhh!" shrieked Donkey.

"Ahhhh!" shrieked the ogress.

"What'd you do with the Princess?" Donkey demanded.

"Shhhhh! I'm the Princess. It's me. In this body," the ogress replied in Fiona's voice.

"Oh my God. You ate the Princess!!! Can you hear me?!" shouted Donkey, addressing the ogress's stomach.

"Shhh! I've been this way as long as I can remember. It only happens when the sun goes down.

By night one way, by day another. This shall be the norm. Until you find true love's first kiss. And then take love's true form,

"That's why I have to marry Lord Farquaad tomorrow before the sun sets and he sees me... like this."

"Princess, how about if you don't marry Farquaad? You know, you're kind of an ogre and Shrek – well, you've got a lot in common," Donkey suggested.

Take a good look at me, Donkey. I mean really..."

Shrek stopped at the door of the mill with a flower for Fiona and overheard the Princess talking to Donkey

"...who could ever love a beast so hideous and ugly? And princess and ugly don't go together. That's why I can't stay here with Shrek. I have to marry my true love. It's the only way to break the spell." Stunned and hurt, Shrek dropped the flower and walked away.

Fiona made Donkey promise not to tell anyone her secret. When he left, Fiona found the flower and lay awake, picking off the petals one by one. "I tell him, I tell him not, I tell him," she chanted and eventually came to a decision. She headed for the door in search of Shrek.

As the ogress stepped outside, the sun rose, and she turned back into a beautiful princess. "Shrek! There's something I have to tell you." She stopped, noticing that Shrek looked mighty mad.

"You don't have to tell me anything," he said, "I heard enough last night – 'Who could love such a hideous and ugly beast?'"

"I thought that wouldn't matter to you," Fiona said.

"Well it does," Shrek told her.

They were interrupted by the approach of Lord Farquaad and his army. "Here's the deed to your swamp, ogre, cleared out as agreed.

"Forgive me, Princess, for startling you," Farquaad continued, "but I have never seen such a radiant beauty before. Princess Fiona, I ask your hand in marriage."

"I accept," she replied, glaring at Shrek.

"Excellent! I'll start the plans, for tomorrow we wed!" Farquaad declared.

"No, let's get married today, before sunset." Fiona blurted out.

"Oh, anxious are we?" asked Farquaad. "You're right, the sooner the better."

Sadly Shrek returned to his swamp and sat down to eat, but he had no appetite. Then he heard a noise outside and went to investigate.

"Donkey! What are you doing?" he shouted.

"You of all people should recognise a wall when you see one!" Donkey replied.

"Well – yeah," said Shrek, "But it's supposed to go around my swamp, not through it."

"It is. Around your half. That's your half and this is my half. I helped rescue the princess and I get half the booty," Donkey explained.

"This is my swamp!" Shrek exploded.

"With you it's always me, me,

me. You are mean to me, you insult me and you don't appreciate anything that I do," Donkey complained.

"Oh yeah – well if I treated you so bad how come you came back?" Shrek demanded.

"There you are doing it again. Just like you did to Fiona. And all she ever did was like you. Maybe even love you," Donkey continued.

"Love me?" asked Shrek, astonished, "She said I was ugly! A hideous creature!"

"She wasn't talking about you!" Donkey explained.

"She wasn't talking about me? Well, what DID she say about me then?" Shrek asked.

"Why don't you ask her yourself?" Donkey replied.

"The wedding!" Shrek shouted with a start. "We'll never make it in time!"

"Never fear. Where there's a will there's a way... and I have a way," said Donkey. To Shrek's surprise, Dragon flew in. They climbed on her back and she flew them to the cathedral in Duloc.

"People of Duloc, we gather here today to bear witness to the union of our new King and Queen."

Fiona glanced nervously at the window, where the sun was going down, and interrupted the Bishop, "Um... Excuse me... ah... Could we just skip ahead to the 'I dos'?"

Farquaad was about to kiss his new bride, when Shrek burst into the cathedral. "I object!" he yelled. "Fiona, you can't marry him! He's just marrying you so he can be King. He's not your true love!"

Farquaad puckered his lips, "Fiona, my love, we're but a kiss away from our happily-ever-after," he said.

Fiona backed away and turned to Shrek. "By night one way, by day another..." she said. "I wanted to show you before..." . As the sun set, she closed her eyes and waited. As Fiona transformed into an ogress, Farquaad's eyes grew wide with shock and revulsion.

But Shrek smiled "Ahhh... that explains a lot!" he said.

"Guards!! I order you to get them out of my sight!" Farquaad shouted, grabbing the crown from the podium. "All this hocus pocus alters nothing.

This marriage is binding and that makes me King!

"Insolent beast. I'll make you regret the day we met!" Farquaad yelled, as the guards dragged Shrek away. "And as for you, my wife! I'll have you locked back in that tower for the rest of your days!!!"

Suddenly the window shattered and Dragon's head appeared.

"Alright," shouted Donkey, sitting astride Dragon, "nobody move. I got a dragon here and I'm not afraid to use it!" And then Dragon swallowed Farquaad in one gulp, spitting out his crown with a belch.

"I love you," said Shrek, turning to Fiona.

"I love you too," she replied. As they kissed, a magical glow surrounded Fiona and she floated up towards the ceiling, then fell back to the ground. She was still an ogress. "I don't understand," she said, "I'm supposed to be beautiful."

"But you are beautiful," Shrek told her.

Shrek and Fiona were married in the swamp and all the fairytale creatures and Dulocians joined in the celebrations. When Fiona threw her bouquet, it was intercepted by Dragon, who turned to Donkey batting her eyelids.

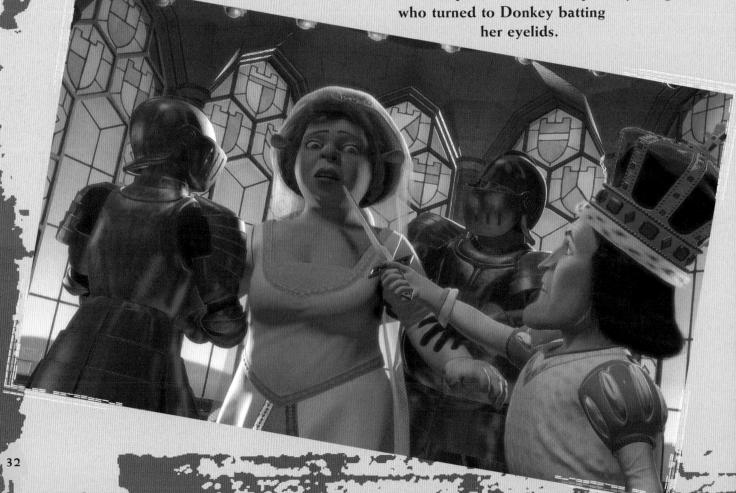

START

Big Bug Race Game

1	1	1	1				
2	2	2	2	3 — You are chased by a frog run forward to 8 — 4	5	6	7
3	3 — A slug is blocking the path. Miss a turn	3	4	5	6	7 — 8	9
4 — A slug is blocking the path. Miss a turn	4	5	6	7	8	9 — 10 You get caught in a spider's web. Miss a turn.	11
5	6	7	8	9	10	11 — 12	13

41	40	39	38	37 — Shrek is peckish! Go back to 38 and hide under a rock	36	35 — 34	33
42	42	41	40	39	38	37 — 36	35 — Shrek is peckish! Go back to 30 and hide under a rock
43	43	43 — Shrek is peckish! Go back to 38 and hide under a rock — 42	41	40	39 — 38	37
44	44	44	44	43	42	41 — 40	39
45	45	45	45				

FINISH

A game for four players, you will need a die. Trace or photocopy the bug counters and stick them onto thin card, or use plastic counters in colours to match the bugs. Each player takes a turn to throw the die and moves his or her counter according to the number thrown. The first to reach the finishing line is the winner.

9	10	11	12	13	14	15	16	17	20
								A slug is blocking the path. Miss a turn	
11	12	13	14 You get caught in a spider's web. Miss a turn.	15	16	17	20 A slug is blocking the path. Miss a turn	21	21
13	14	15	16	17	20	21	22	22	22
15	16	17	20	21 You are chased by a frog run forward to 23	22	23	23	23	23
					24	24	24	24	
31	30	29 You get caught in a spider's web. Miss a turn.	28	27	26	25	25	25	25 Shrek is peckish! Go back to 20 and hide under a rock
33	32	31	30	29	28	27	26 You are chased by a frog run forward to 28	26	26
35	34	33	32	31	30	29	28	27	27
37	36 You get caught in a spider's web. Miss a turn.	35	34	33	32	31	30	29	28

Meet the In-laws

Once upon a time, in a kingdom far, far away, the King and Queen were blessed with a beautiful baby girl. And throughout the land everyone was happy... until the sun went down and they saw that she was cursed with a frightful enchantment that took hold each and every night. Desperate, they sought the help of a fairy godmother who had them lock the young princess in a tower to await the kiss of the handsome Prince Charming. It was he who would chance the perilous journey through blistering cold and scorching desert, travelling for many days and nights, risking life and limb to reach the Dragon's Keep.

Prince Charming stormed the castle and removed his helmet, revealing a hairnet. He took it off and shook out his golden locks. Entering Fiona's room in the tallest tower, he pulled back the gossamer curtains to find a wolf relaxing in the bed.

"Princess Fiona?" the prince gasped. He had heard that she was enchanted, but this was not at all what he had expected.

"No!" the wolf replied.

"Oh thank heavens... Where is she?" Charmng asked.

"She's on her honeymoon," said the wolf.

"With whom??" the prince spluttered.

Shrek carried his new bride over the threshold of Hansel's Honeymoon Hideaway, smashing the doorframe on the way in. The newly-weds shared many romantic moments – shaving together in the mornings, frolicking on the beach, running through flower-filled meadows under a hail of pitchforks and making bubbles in the mud hot tub.

Shrek sighed, as he and Fiona returned to the swamp. "It's so good to be home, just you and me. "Opening the door he found Donkey sitting in his favourite chair.

"Donkey, shouldn't you be getting home to Dragon?" Fiona asked hopefully.

"Dragon's been all moody lately, so I thought I'd move back in with you guys,"

Donkey said, with what he hoped was a winning smile.

"But, Donkey, Fiona and I are married now. We need time together ALONE," Shrek tried to explain.

As Shrek and Fiona opened the door to get rid of Donkey, they were surprised by a fanfare of trumpets.

"Dearest Princess Fiona," read a page, "You are hereby summoned to the Kingdom of Far, Far Away for a royal ball in celebration of your marriage at which time the King will bestow his royal blessing upon you and your Prince Charming. Love, the King and Queen of Far, Far Away, aka Mum and Dad."

"We are not going!" Shrek declared. "Trust me, it's a bad idea. That's final!"

The following morning Shrek reluctantly loaded his suitcase onto the carriage. Donkey jumped on top of the luggage.

"Hey, c'mon, Shrek, we don't want to hit traffic," he said. The fairytale creatures waved goodbye then ran into Shrek's house to party.

"Are we there yet?" asked Donkey as they passed a sign reading '700 miles to Far Away'.

"Are we there yet?" asked Donkey as they drove through the mountains past a sign reading '200 miles to Away'.

"Are we there yet?" asked Donkey as they travelled through a forest past a sign reading '100 miles to Far, Far Away'.

"NO WE ARE NOT!" Shrek yelled.

"This is taking forever," Donkey moaned, "there ain't no inflight movie or nothing."

Shrek gritted his teeth, "The Kingdom of Far Far Away, Donkey, that's where we're going... FAR... FAR... AWAY!!"

Finally, the carriage entered the city.

Shrek and Fiona smiled nervously at each other as they pulled up outside the castle. Crowds clapped and cheered either side of the red carpet, while the King and Queen waited expectantly at the entrance. A herald swung open the door of the carriage.

"Announcing the long-awaited return of the beautiful Princess Fiona and her new husband," he cried. The cheering was quickly replaced by gasps as Shrek and Fiona emerged.

"So... you still think this was a good idea?" Shrek asked Fiona, glancing at the stunned onlookers.

"Who on earth are they?! Wasn't she supposed to kiss Prince Charming and break the spell?" the King stuttered, as Shrek and Fiona approached.

The Queen tried to make the best of the situation, "Well, he's no Prince Charming but they do look happy together."

The atmosphere was tense over dinner that night. "I suppose any grandchildren I could expect from you would be..." the King began.

"Ogres... yes!" Shrek replied.

"Not that there's anything wrong with that," the Queen added quickly.

"No, of course not, assuming you don't eat your own young," the King declared.

"Oh no, we prefer the ones who've been locked away in a tower," Shrek replied angrily.

The King was furious. "I only did that because I loved her," he bellowed.

"It's so nice to have the family together for dinner," said the Queen.

41

Fiona ran from the table to her bedroom. She stepped out onto the balcony and a tear fell onto the railing. Suddenly a large bubble appeared. Inside it was the Fairy Godmother.

"Ahhh!!!" cried the Fairy Godmother when she saw that Fiona was an ogress. "I'm your Fairy Godmother," she explained.

"With just a wave of my magic wand,
Your troubles will be gone,
With a flick of the wrist and just a flash,
You'll land a prince with a ton of cash."

Enchanted pieces of furniture started to dance around the room, surrounding Fiona. They were interrupted by a knock at the door and Shrek and Donkey burst in.

"Ah... Fairy Godmother, furniture... I'd like you to meet my husband, Shrek,"

The Fairy Godmother stared in shock. "Your husband? When did this happen? That can't be right!" She turned to leave, then offered her card to Fiona. "Remember, if you ever need me... Happiness... It's just a teardrop away."

Shrek grabbed the card, "Thanks but we've got all the happiness we need."

"Fiona was supposed to choose the prince we picked out for her. Instead our daughter has married a monster," the King moaned to his wife that night, as he paced up and down in front of the bedroom window. Suddenly the Fairy Godmother's carriage appeared outside. The King rushed out onto the balcony, quickly closing the shutters behind him.

"Get in!" the Fairy Godmother ordered, "We need to talk. You remember my son, Prince Charming? He endured blistering winds and scorching desert! He climbed to the highest room of the tallest tower... and what did he find? Some wolf telling him that HIS princess is already married! We made a deal, Harold, and I assume you don't want me to go back on my part! So Fiona and Charming WILL be together. It's what's best... not only for your daughter but for your kingdom!" The king was shoved back out onto his balcony and the carriage zoomed off.

Late that night the King wrapped himself in a cloak and rode to The Poison Apple. He went into the gloomy bar and whispered to the ugly stepsister behind the counter, "I need to have someone taken care of. He's an ogre." She directed him to a room at the back. A pair of eyes glinted in the darkness.

"I'm told you're the one to talk to about an ogre problem," the King said hesitantly, handing over a large sack of gold.

Unable to sleep, Shrek wandered around Fiona's bedroom. He flicked open young Fiona's diary and read, 'Dad says I'm going away for a while. And Mum says, when I'm old enough, my handsome Prince Charming will rescue me and bring me back to my family.' Hearing someone outside, Shrek opened the bedroom door and was surprised to see King Harold.

"I wanted to apologise for my despicable behaviour," he told Shrek. "Would you join me for a morning hunt? A little father-son time. Shall we say 7:30 by the old oak?"

Next morning Shrek and Donkey were looking for the old oak tree when they heard a purring sound. Suddenly a cat armed with a sword jumped out from behind a tree.

"Ha ha! Fear me... if you DARE!!!" it hissed.

"It's a cat," Shrek said playfully, "c'mere little kitty, kitty, kitty."

Puss In Boots leapt out of his boots and dug his claws into Shrek's thigh. He disappeared inside the ogre's shirt, then ripped his way out. Shrek grabbed the cat by the scruff of his neck.

"Please, it was nothing personal, Señor," Puss pleaded, "I was doing it for my family. The

King offered me much in gold and I have a litter of brothers."

"Whoa, whoa, Fiona's father paid you to do this?" asked Shrek dismayed.

"Oh come on Shrek," said Donkey trying to comfort him, "Almost everybody that meets you wants to kill you."

Shrek stared at his reflection in the stream. "Maybe Fiona would have been better off if I were some sort of Prince Charming," he said sadly. "I just wish I could make her happy."

Suddenly he remembered something. He took a card from his pocket. 'Happiness... A teardrop away,' he read. "Donkey, think of the saddest thing that's ever happened to you."

"Well, there was the time that old farmer tried to sell me for some magic beans. Then this fool had a party and all the guests tried to pin the tail on me. Then they beat me with a stick shouting 'piñata'..." Donkey began.

"No, Donkey, I need you to cry," said Shrek. Suddenly Puss stepped on Donkey's hoof with the heel of his boot. "UUGGGGHHHH," Donkey yelled, a tear coming to his eye. Shrek quickly held the card under it.

The teardrop turned into a bubble and from inside came the voice of the Fairy Godmother, "I'm either away from my desk or with a client, but if you come by the office we'll be glad to make you a personal appointment. Have a happy ever after."

"Are you up for a little quest, Donkey?" asked Shrek.

"Ogre, I am obliged to accompany you until I have saved your life, as you have spared me mine," Puss said, jumping to his feet.

Donkey gave him a withering look, "I'm sorry," he said, "The position of annoying talking animal has already been taken. Let's go, Shrek."

"Fairy Godmother is not in," the receptionist told Shrek, Donkey and Puss when they arrived at her factory. Then they heard her voice over the intercom, demanding coffee and a sandwich.

"We're from the Union," Shrek said, "We represent the workers in all magical industries. We'll just take a look around."

Shrek disguised himself as a janitor and, with Donkey and Puss hidden in the janitor's cart, he made his way to the potion room. Puss climbed up rows of shelves packed with bottles.

"Look for Handsome," Shrek suggested.

"Sorry, no Handsome," Puss told him. "How about Happily Ever After? It says 'Beauty Divine' on the label." Suddenly alarms went off and lights started flashing.

"Run!" Shrek yelled. The trio managed to escape from the factory with the bottle and headed into the woods.

"Everything is accounted for except for one potion," the receptionist told the Fairy Godmother, after checking the stocks. The Fairy Godmother grabbed the list from him.

"I do believe we can make this work to our advantage," she said.

"Boss, in case there is something wrong with the potion allow me to take the first sip," offered Puss.

Donkey snatched the bottle, "If there's going to be any animal testing, I'm going to do it," he said, taking a swig. They waited expectantly but nothing happened.

"Maybe it doesn't work on donkeys," said Shrek, downing the potion.

Storm clouds gathered and they ran to a disused barn to shelter from the rain. Donkey started to feel dizzy and promptly passed out. Then Shrek got woozy and crashed to the ground. A puff of magical blue smoke burst through the door and windows of the barn. At the same moment, blue smoke burst from Fiona's window back at the castle.

Cookie Couples

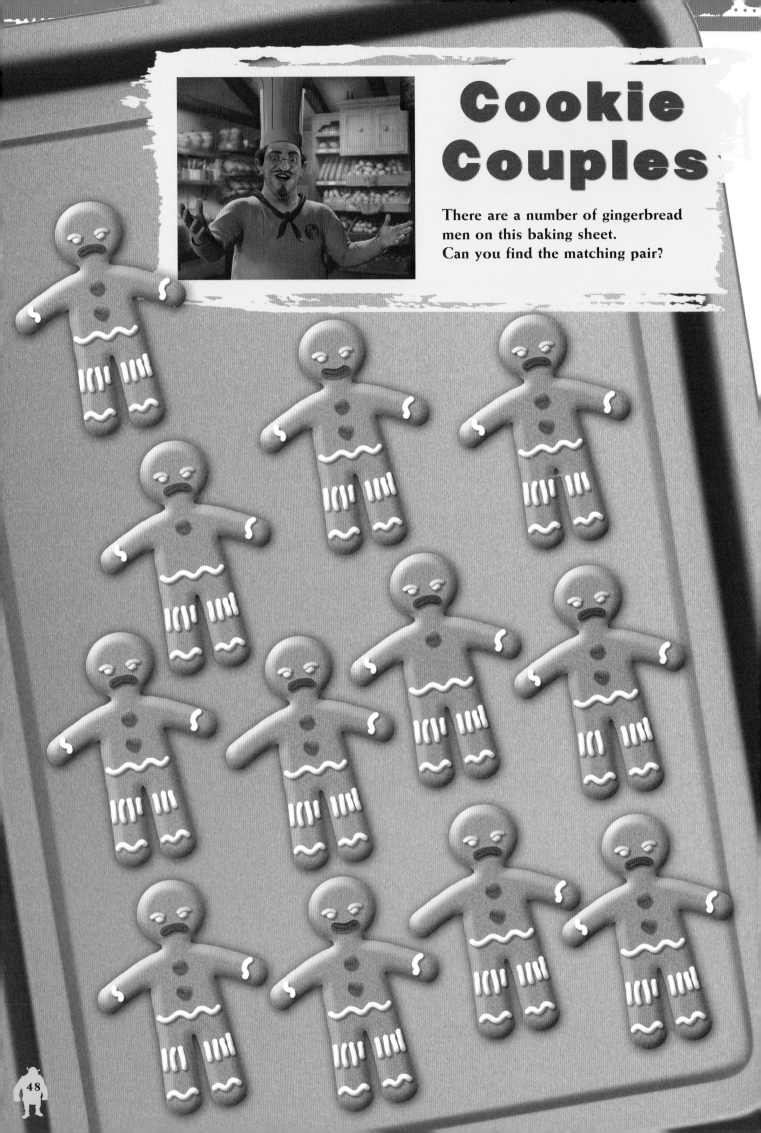

There are a number of gingerbread men on this baking sheet. Can you find the matching pair?

Monster munch

Eyeballs a l'Ogre

4 hard-boiled eggs
2 tablespoons mayonnaise
8 green olives stuffed with pimento

Cut thin slices off each end of the boiled eggs so they will stand up, then cut each one in half through the middle. Scoop out the yolks and mix with mayonnaise. Spoon the mixture back into the egg whites and top with a stuffed olive.

Cheesy worms

Spaghetti
A carton of cheese sauce

Break the spaghetti into four pieces and cook as instructed on the packet. Heat the cheese sauce and add to the spaghetti when cooked.

Bug-infested slime

A packet of green jelly
Some jelly bug sweets

Make up the jelly, using a little extra water (an extra 1 fluid ounce per pint), so the jelly is not set too firmly, and pour it into a large shallow dish. When the jelly has set, decorate it with jelly bugs.

Pond water punch with floating flies

Limeade
Grenadine syrup
Raisins (or jelly Sweets)

Half fill an ice cube tray and fill with water and freeze, then add a couple of raisins (or jelly bugs). Fill he rest of the way with water and freeze again.

Pour the limeade into a glass with a little grenadine syrup and the ice cubes.

Safety First

Ask an adult for help when using sharp knifes and boiling water.

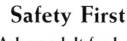

Happily Ogre After

When Shrek woke up the following morning, he was surrounded by three pretty young women. "Oww. My head...," he groaned. "Here, I fetched you a pail of water," said Jill. As Shrek reached for the pail, he was shocked to see two human hands. He looked at his reflection in the water. He was HANDSOME!

"Gorgeous!" said Jill, while the other two maids nodded in agreement.

"Have you ladies seen my donkey?" Shrek asked them.

A beautiful, white steed appeared in the doorway. "Who are you calling Donkey?" he demanded, "I'm a stallion baby! I can whinny. I can count. That's some quality potion."

Puss read the back of the bottle, "To make the effects of this potion permanent, the drinker must obtain his true love's kiss by midnight," he said.

"Pick me! I'll be your true love," the three maids all insisted, as they tried to kiss Shrek.

"Look, ladies, I already have a true love," he told them, backing away. "Look out, Princess, here comes the new me!"

Shrek cut a dashing figure as he rode into town on his noble steed. "Tell Princess Fiona her husband, Sir Shrek, is here to see her," he told a guard at the castle entrance.

Meanwhile, Fiona was washing her face. She saw her reflection in the mirror. She was BEAUTIFUL. Hearing her screams of shock, Shrek rushed into the castle. He spotted a caped figure standing in front of a window.

"Fiona!" he cried.

"Hello handsome," said the Fairy Godmother.

Hearing Shrek call her name, Fiona ran down the hall. She saw a man silhouetted on the balcony of a nearby room. "Shrek?!" she gasped in amazement.

"Aye, Fiona, it is me," replied Prince Charming.

"What happened to your voice?" Fiona asked suspiciously.

"The potion changed a lot of things, but not the way I feel about you," Prince Charming told her. He had fooled Fiona into thinking he was Handsome Shrek.

Across the courtyard Shrek watched as Fiona and Prince Charming embraced. He shouted her name, but she couldn't hear him.

"Don't you think you've already messed her life up enough?" asked the Fairy Godmother. "She's finally found the prince of her dreams. It's time you stopped living in a fairytale, Shrek. She's a Princess and you're an ogre. That's something no amount of potion is ever going to change."

Shrek walked sadly down the castle steps to Donkey and Puss and they headed for The Poison Apple.

"I can't believe you're going to walk away from the best thing that's happened to you," Donkey said, as they downed their drinks.

"What choice do I have?" moaned Shrek, "She loves that pretty boy, Prince Charming."

Suddenly the door burst open and the King walked in, but he didn't recognise Shrek and Donkey. He slipped through a door at the back where the Fairy Godmother was waiting with Prince Charming.

"You'd better have a good reason for dragging us down here," the Fairy Godmother told the King.

"Yes, you see Fiona isn't really warming up to Prince Charming," the King explained, "I mean you can't force someone to fall in love."

"I beg to differ. I do it all the time," said the Fairy Godmother, giving the King a potion bottle. "Have Fiona drink this and she'll fall in love with the first man she kisses, which will be Charming." But the King refused.

"If you remember, I helped you with your happily ever after and I can take it away just as easily," the Fairy Godmother threatened him. "Anyway, we have to go... I need to do Charming's hair before the ball."

"Thank you mother," said Charming.

"MOTHER?!" exclaimed Donkey.

The Fairy Godmother turned to go and spotted Shrek and Donkey spying through the window. "The Ogre! Stop them! Thieves, bandits!" she shouted.

Back at the swamp, the fairytale creatures were watching TV. "Tonight on Knights we've got a white bronco heading into the forest," said the announcer, showing highlights of Shrek, Puss and Donkey's arrest. The fairytale creatures didn't realise that the prisoner being dragged away was Shrek, until they recognised his voice shouting, "Find Princess Fiona. Tell her I'm her husband, Shrek." Confused, they stared at the TV, unable to believe their ears.

At the castle, the King prepared two cups of tea. Reluctantly, he uncorked the potion and stirred it into one of the cups. "How about a cup of tea before the ball?" he asked Fiona.

"I'm not going," Fiona told him.

"But the whole kingdom's turned out to celebrate your marriage," the King tried to persuade her.

"There's just one problem," Fiona replied, looking down at Prince Charming from her window, "That's not my husband!"

"He is a bit different, but people change for the ones they love. You'd be surprised how much I changed for your mother. Why not give him another chance? You might find you like this new Shrek," the King said guiltily.

"But it's the old one I fell in love with Dad, I'd give anything to have him back." Fiona reached for her tea, but the King stopped her.

"That's mine. Decaf," he said quickly.

Shrek, Donkey and Puss found themselves shackled to the wall in a prison cell.

"I must hold on, before I go totally mad," Puss said to himself. He looked up to see the fairytale creatures peering down at them through a grate. "Too late," he added.

The Three Little Pigs blew the grate off the cell and lowered Pinocchio down. They swung him back and forth but he couldn't quite reach Shrek. Gingy jumped onto Pinocchio's back.

"Tell a lie," said Shrek.

"Something crazy, like I'm wearing ladies' underwear," Donkey suggested.

"I'm wearing ladies' underwear," Pinocchio repeated. Nothing happened.

"Are you?" asked Shrek.

"I most certainly am not," Pinocchio replied, as his nose grew. Gingy checked Pinocchio's shorts and found a pink thong. Pinocchio's nose grew longer and longer until

Gingy was just inches from Shrek. He unlocked the shackles and Shrek, Donkey and Puss fell to the ground.

"We've gotta stop that kiss! I can't let them do this to Fiona," Shrek declared.

"We'll never get in. The castle is guarded and there's a moat and everything," said Puss.

Then Shrek had an idea. "Do you still know the Muffin Man?" he asked Gingy.

"Sure, he's down on Drury Lane," Gingy replied.

"We're going to need flour," Shrek told him, "lots and lots of flour."

So Shrek and Gingy set off to find the Muffin Man.

"Fire up the ovens, Muffin Man, we've got a big order to fill," Gingy said. Soon the ovens were blazing and the Muffin Man was mixing ingredients in huge vats. Suddenly the house was struck by lightning and strange laughter came from inside. "It's alive," cried Gingy.

That evening in Far Far Away, people ran for cover as a huge shadow loomed over them. Shrek was riding on the shoulders of a giant gingerbread man, while Gingy rode on Shrek's shoulders.

"Go, baby, go," shouted Gingy.

At the castle, Charming waved to the crowd as he and Fiona approached the ballroom.

"Shrek, what are you doing?" demanded Fiona.

"Just playing the part," Charming replied.

"Is that glitter on your lips?" Fiona asked suspiciously.

"Mmm," said Charming, "cherry flavoured. Want a taste?"

Fiona turned away in disgust. Seeing Fiona storm off, the Fairy Godmother took to the stage. "Ladies and gentlemen," she announced, "I'd like to dedicate this song to Princess Fiona and Prince Shrek."

The spotlight landed on Fiona and, with all eyes on her, she felt obliged to join Charming on the dance floor.

"All right big fella, let's crash this party," Shrek yelled.

"Man the catapults!" shouted the captain of the guards as the giant cookie approached the castle. A fireball hit the giant gingerbread man in the chest and set fire to one of his gumdrop buttons. Enraged he kicked the burning gumdrop over the castle wall. It landed on one of the catapults and smashed it.

"Man the cauldrons!" ordered the Captain.

The giant gingerbread man jumped into the moat and grabbed the drawbridge, trying to pull it down. The guards poured an enormous bottle of milk into a massive cauldron and heated it up, then they poured the steaming milk onto the giant cookie. His arms started to dissolve then he groaned and fell backwards into the moat. Shrek leapt through a crack in the drawbridge, slid down the chain and took out the guards at the bottom. Then he lowered the drawbridge and the fairytale creatures raced into the castle.

Shrek jumped onto Donkey's back and they headed for the ballroom, while Puss fought off the guards. They burst in just as Charming was about to kiss Fiona.

"STOP!!!" yelled Shrek, "Back away from my wife."

"Shrek?" gasped Fiona.

"She's taken the potion, kiss her now!" the Fairy Godmother ordered. Before Fiona could react, Charming had planted a huge kiss on her lips. Fiona stepped towards him, putting her hands on his face, then headbutted him, knocking him unconscious.

The Fairy Godmother was livid. "Harold, you were supposed to give her the potion!" she shouted at the King.

"I guess I gave her the wrong tea," he said.

"Mummy," Charming called out, as he staggered to his feet.

"MUMMY?!" exclaimed Fiona.

The Fairy Godmother flew up into the air and raised her wand, summoning all her evil powers. As she released her wicked magic, Shrek pushed Fiona to safety, then the King dived in front of Shrek. The King took the full blast, but the magic bounced off his shiny armour straight back to the Fairy Godmother, who exploded, leaving just her glasses behind.

Fiona and Shrek rushed over to the King. All that remained was his armour. From inside came a ribbit sound and out jumped a frog.

"Harold?" asked the Queen.

"Dad?" gasped Fiona.

The frog turned to Fiona, "I'd hoped you'd never see me like this," he croaked.

"Man! And he gave you a hard time!" Donkey said to Shrek.

"He's right," the frog agreed. "I'm sorry, I only wanted what was best for Fiona, but I can see now she already has it. Shrek, Fiona, will you accept an old frog's apologies, and my blessing?"

The Queen scooped up the frog. "I'm sorry, Lillian. I wish I could be the man you deserve," he said.

"You're more that man today than you ever were... warts and all," the Queen replied.

The clock chimed midnight. Shrek took Fiona in his arms.

"Fiona, is this what you want, to be this way forever? If you kiss me now we can stay like this" he said.

"You'd do that for me?" she asked.

"Yes," Shrek said.

Fiona looked at him, then back at her parents.

"I want what any Princess wants... to live happily ever after... with the ogre I married."

As the last chime sounded, Shrek and Fiona braced themselves and their bodies were transformed back into their ogre selves.

Donkey was suspended over the crowd as his transformation began. His horseshoes popped off, his mane became a mohawk and his ears grew. He looked sadly at Shrek as he floated back to the floor.

Shrek smiled "Hey, you still look like a noble steed to me," he said.

"Now where were we?" Fiona asked Shrek.

"Oh, I remember," Shrek replied. They kissed and the crowd applauded. Then Puss and Donkey launched into a duet to kick the party off.